Butts on THE RUN!

Dawn McMillan

Illustrated by Ross Kinnaird

Dover Publications
Garden City, New York

Today is **race** day!
I'm here at the start.

I **SO** want to win —
I have hope in my heart.

I'm ready ...
I'm steady ...
And off I go!

But ...

... I'm coming in last
because my butt is so **slow**.

My legs are long.
My knees are **strong**.
But my butt needs something
to move it along.

Like ...

...A **BIG** shiny engine
that makes a jet ROAR.

Or a high-flying kite
to make my butt
soar.

Balloons perhaps,
tied all about.

They will propel me
when the air **rushes** out.

Or a rocket butt **BLAST** — I'd never be last!

And if I were followed by *bees*, my butt would run **FAST!**

My cousin is Tom.
He runs **slowly** too.
"Tom," I say,

"I know what to do!"

I know that **bends**
are good for rear ends.

And kicks

here and **there**,

with one leg in the air.

Yes, step **up** and step **down** …
1, 2 and 3, 4.

A **lunge** and a **plunge** …
and then we do it some more.

Oops!

There's the odd little slipup
that sounds like a **hiccup**.

But what's that we hear?
Is it a **cheer?**

There's whooping and hollering.
Seems we have a following.

WHAT A HULLABALOO!

They're having fun too!

So now Tom and I go running for **fun**.
Down the footpath, past all the trees.
I'm out in front, moving with ease.
With my new **secret** weapon —

cabbage and peas!

And I know ...

My butt could run **FAST**
in all sorts of races
all over the world,
in wonderful places.

Like ...

Through city streets, and on riverbanks too.

Up on tall cliffs with the very **best** view.

A **mud** run perhaps, a race in the **rain**.

Around the lakeshore, and back again.

A race in the desert? Now that would be **fun**.
With a **strong** butt, that could be done.

In **cold** places I know we could race in the *snow*.

I could race high, right up to the sky.

To race by the sea would really suit me.

Yes ... I'd like to be *famous*.
A world **racing** star!
But my butt isn't keen to travel too far.

So ...

Tom and I enter a cross-country race.
Over **hills** and through **streams**,
near our homeplace.

And I'm over the gate!
But Tom's running late!
Along a farm track!
I'm too near the back!

I need more grunt to get to the front.

The line's up ahead! My face is **RED!**

My muscles are pumping! My butt is jumping!

A dash for the line. I'm feeling **fine.**

And ...

... Yes!

My butt can run! My butt has WON!

But wait ... What's that I hear?

Guess who has won
by the tip of his ear?

About the author

Hi, I'm Dawn McMillan. I'm from Waiomu, a small coastal village on the western side of the Coromandel Peninsula in New Zealand. I live with my husband, Derek, and our cat, Lola. I write some sensible stories and lots of crazy stories! I love creating quirky characters and hope you enjoy reading about them.

About the illustrator

Hi. I'm Ross. I love to draw. When I'm not drawing, or being cross with my computer, I love most things involving the sea and nature. I also work from a little studio in my garden surrounded by birds and trees. I live in Auckland, New Zealand. I hope you like reading this book as much as I enjoyed illustrating it.

Bibliographical Note

This Dover edition, first published in 2023, is an unabridged republication of the work published as *My Bum's on THE RUN!* by Oratia Media Ltd., Auckland, New Zealand, in 2023. The text has been Americanized for this edition.

International Standard Book Number

ISBN-13: 978-0-486-85135-8
ISBN-10: 0-486-85135-4

Manufactured in the United States of America
85135402   2023
www.doverpublications.com